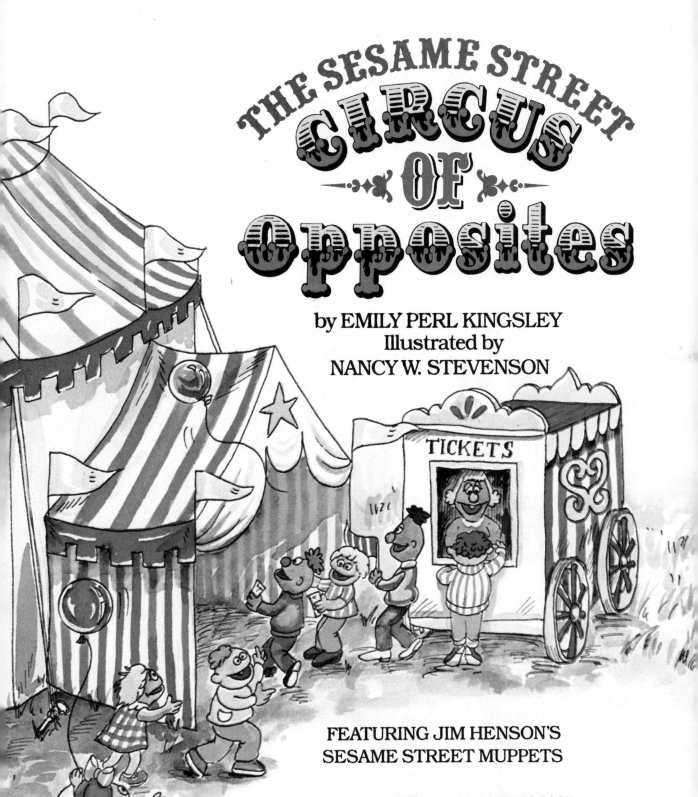

THE SESAME STREET CIRCUS OF Opposites

by EMILY PERL KINGSLEY
Illustrated by
NANCY W. STEVENSON

FEATURING JIM HENSON'S
SESAME STREET MUPPETS

A SESAME STREET/GOLDEN PRESS BOOK
Published by Western Publishing Company, Inc.
in conjunction with Children's Television Workshop.

It was time for the circus to begin.

"Welcome, welcome, welcome, ladies and gentlemen, boys and girls!" cried Guy Smiley, the Ringmaster. "Welcome to the Most Wonderful Show on Earth... THE SESAME STREET CIRCUS OF OPPOSITES!"

Guy Smiley blew his whistle.

"And here comes the circus parade!" he shouted. "Look! It's Big Bird, riding on a BIG elephant! And here comes Little Bird, riding on a LITTLE elephant!"

"Let me direct your attention to the one and only Prairie Dawn," announced Guy Smiley. "She's the daring young girl on the sliding wire. There she is, way UP in the air!"

Prairie slid down the wire and jumped to the ground. "Now Prairie Dawn is safely DOWN on the ground. Let's hear it for Prairie!"

"Yay!" cheered the audience.

"And now, everyone," said Guy Smiley, "watch carefully as fearless Grover is shot from a cannon! I think he is ready. Yes, fearless Grover is now IN the cannon!"

BOOM!
"Look at him go!" shouted Guy Smiley.
"Fearless Grover is OUT of the cannon!"
"Aaaaiiiiieeeee!" cried Grover.

Grover flew through the air.

"Ahhh," he said to himself, "this is so much fun! I am flying through the air in my beautiful shiny CLEAN silver-and-white flying suit. Uh-oh! I think I am going to land now."

"Yaaaggghhh!" shouted Grover, as he fell into a big, deep pile of sawdust.

"Oh, no!" he cried. "Now my beautiful silver-and-white flying suit is all DIRTY!"

Next came the parade of clowns.
Deena was a very TALL clown.
Elmo was a very SHORT clown.
Telly Monster was a very FAT clown.
Pearl was a very THIN clown.

"And now, boys and girls," called Guy Smiley, "watch one of the most fantastic acts in the circus. The incredible Herry Monster is now DRY. But see what happens when he dives from that platform into this pail of water!"

"He did it!" shouted Guy Smiley. "He dived right into the pail of water, and now Herry is all WET!"

"Ladies and gentlemen," Guy Smiley announced, "in the center ring our brave trick riders will now perform amazing feats. Just look at Ernie. He is standing ON the horse.

"Uh-oh. Bert seems to be OFF his horse."

Betty Lou and Cookie Monster were watching the circus from the stands.

"Hey, Betty Lou," said Cookie Monster. "That sure is a FULL box of popcorn."

"Would you like some popcorn, Cookie?" asked Betty Lou.

"Wow!" said Betty Lou when she saw her EMPTY
box of popcorn.

"And now the Terrific Tumblers!" cried Guy Smiley.

"Observe this amazing demonstration of balance and skill! Featuring our own Rodeo Rosie on the BOTTOM, and the fabulous Granny Fanny Nesslerode on TOP!"

"Now The Sesame Street Circus of Opposites presents the courageous Count on the HIGH wire!" cried Guy Smiley.

"And on the LOW wire is the fantastic Ftatateeta."

Finally, for the last act of the circus, a small car drove into the center ring. The door opened, and clowns came piling out of the car.

The FIRST clown to climb out of the car was Frazzle.

The LAST clown to climb out was Barkley the dog.

"It's SAD that circus is all over," said Cookie Monster, as he and Betty Lou walked home together.

"I had a great time," said Betty Lou. "I sure am GLAD we went to the circus."

BCDEFGHIJ